Love, Agnes

POSTCARDS FROM AN OCTOPUS

IRENE LATHAM

ILLUSTRATED BY
THEA BAKER

Ⓜ Millbrook Press • Minneapolis

For Charles, MadiLynn, and James—unexpected treasures   —I.L.

For Jamie and Zuri—big, octopus-sized hugs   —T.B.

Thank you to octopus expert Jennifer Mather, Professor at the University of Lethbridge, for reviewing the text and illustrations.

Millbrook Press
A division of Lerner Publishing Group, Inc.
241 First Avenue North
Minneapolis, MN 55401 USA

For reading levels and more information, look up this title at www.lernerbooks.com.

Designed by Emily Harris.
Diagram © Laura Westlund/Independent Picture Service, p. 30.
Main body text set in Mikado 17/23.
Typeface provided by HVD Fonts.
The illustrations in this book were created using mixed media, including collage, acrylic paint, and digital.

Library of Congress Cataloging-in-Publication Data

Names: Latham, Irene, author. | Baker, Thea, illustrator.
Title: Love, Agnes : postcards from an octopus / Irene Latham ; illustrated by Thea Baker.
Description: Minneapolis : Millbrook Press, [2018] | Summary: In California, Agnes, a giant Pacific octopus, pens a series of postcards to strangers from both above and below the pier.
Identifiers: LCCN 2017046875 (print) | LCCN 2017059853 (ebook) | ISBN 9781541524705 (eb pdf) | ISBN 9781512439939 (lb : alk. paper)
Subjects: | CYAC: North Pacific giant octopus—Fiction. | Octopuses—Fiction. | Postcards—Fiction.
Classification: LCC PZ7.L3476 (ebook) | LCC PZ7.L3476 Lo 2018 (print) | DDC [E]—dc23

LC record available at https://lccn.loc.gov/2017046875

Manufactured in the United States of America
1-42255-26120-3/19/2018

One day in the deep dark beneath the pier, an octopus found a large jar. She knew it would make the perfect home. But something was blocking her way.

Dear Nobody,

Mom said I'm not allowed to call you a monster, even though that's what you are. So I'm writing it instead. MONSTER. Things were great until you came along.

Your nothing,

Andrew

Nobody

Seaside Pier

California

The octopus turned bright red. Her arms twitched. She knew she wouldn't be able to rest until she wrote a reply.

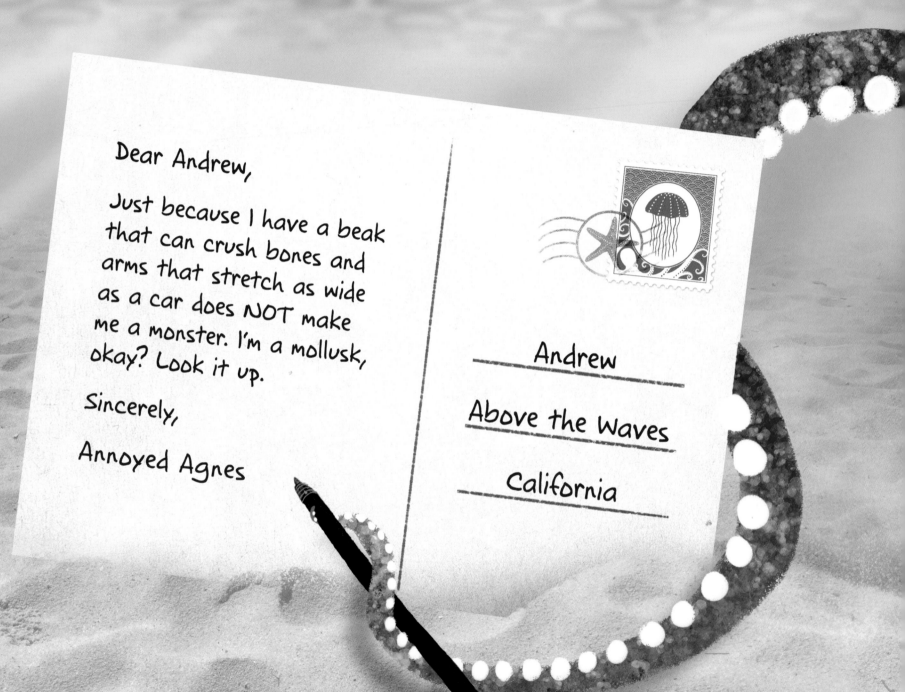

Dear Andrew,

Just because I have a beak that can crush bones and arms that stretch as wide as a car does NOT make me a monster. I'm a mollusk, okay? Look it up.

Sincerely,

Annoyed Agnes

Andrew

Above the Waves

California

Agnes watched the postcard drift away.

She tucked herself into the jar to wait for a tasty crab to scuttle by.

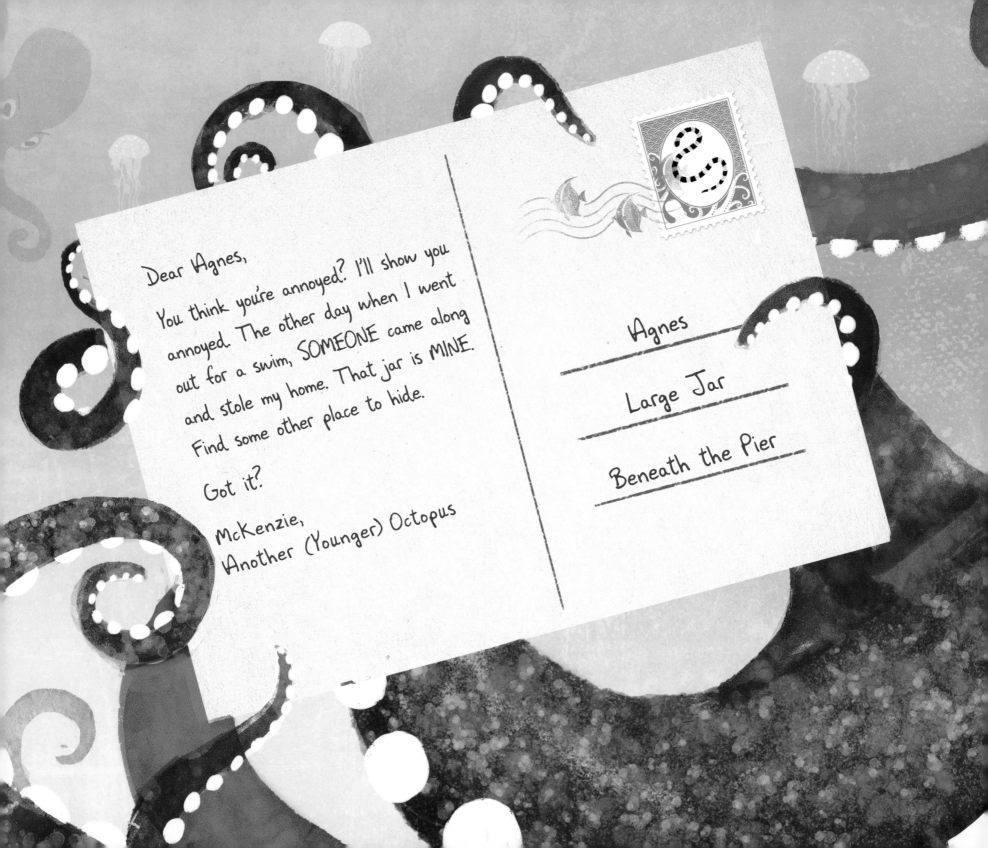

Dear Agnes,

You think you're annoyed? I'll show you annoyed. The other day when I went out for a swim, SOMEONE came along and stole my home. That jar is MINE. Find some other place to hide.

Got it?

McKenzie,
Another (Younger) Octopus

Agnes

Large Jar

Beneath the Pier

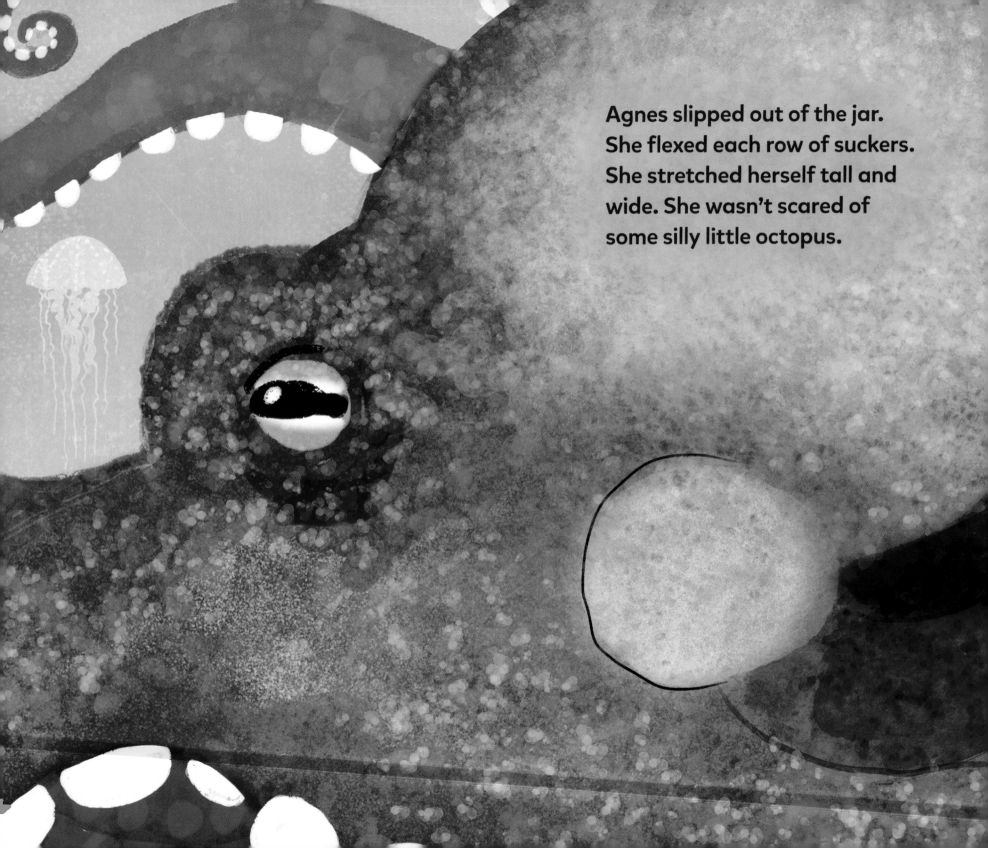

Agnes slipped out of the jar. She flexed each row of suckers. She stretched herself tall and wide. She wasn't scared of some silly little octopus.

Dear McKenzie,

Fine. I'm leaving. I have more important things to do than fight. Besides, this jar stinks. Now I know why.

NOT sincerely,

(Older, Wiser) Agnes

McKenzie

Large Stinky Jar

Beneath the Pier

Agnes glided along the ocean floor until she found a cozy pile of rocks. She knocked on the door not once but eight times. No one answered, so she settled into a crevice and fell asleep. When she woke, this is what she found.

Dear Agnes,

Ahoy! I have an announcement: for all crabs everywhere, I feel it is my duty to inform you that we do not like your arms or your suckers or the way you crunch. Find some other lunch!

—A CRAB HAPPY TO HAVE ESCAPED YOUR SUCKERS

Agnes

Old Rock Pile

Beneath the Pier

Agnes sighed. She wasn't very hungry anyway.

It was time to lay her eggs.

Dear Crab,

Okay, I'll leave you and your friends alone. IF you'll promise me this: BE QUIET. No skittering or scuttling near my nest. My babies need their rest.

Thanks in advance,

Exhausted Agnes

Crabby Crab

Ocean Floor

Beneath the Pier

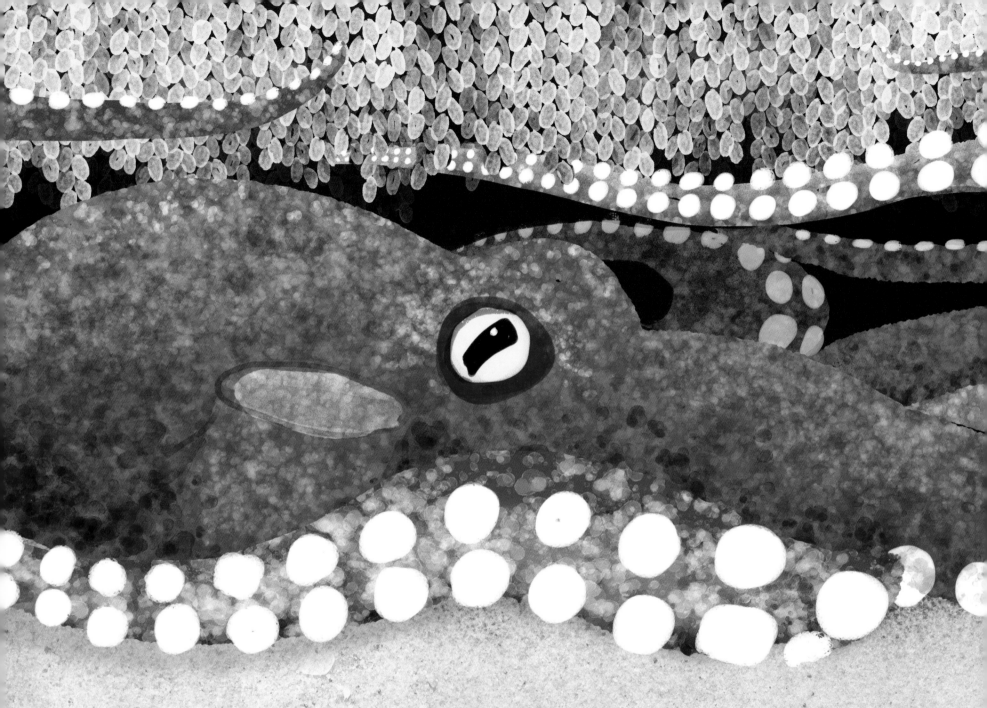

Agnes admired her eggs. She cleaned them and
coddled them. When she looked up from her work,
another postcard had arrived.

Dear Agnes,

You call yourself WISE? Ha! I'M the one who chased YOU out of that jar. No way are you smarter than me.

McKenzie, the Smartest Octopus in the Sea

Agnes

Old Rock Pile

Beneath the Pier

Agnes rolled her eyes. She still knew how to do a thing or two. She jetted superfast across a current. When a dogfish followed too close, she blasted it with a cloud of ink.

When the water cleared, what did she see floating by?

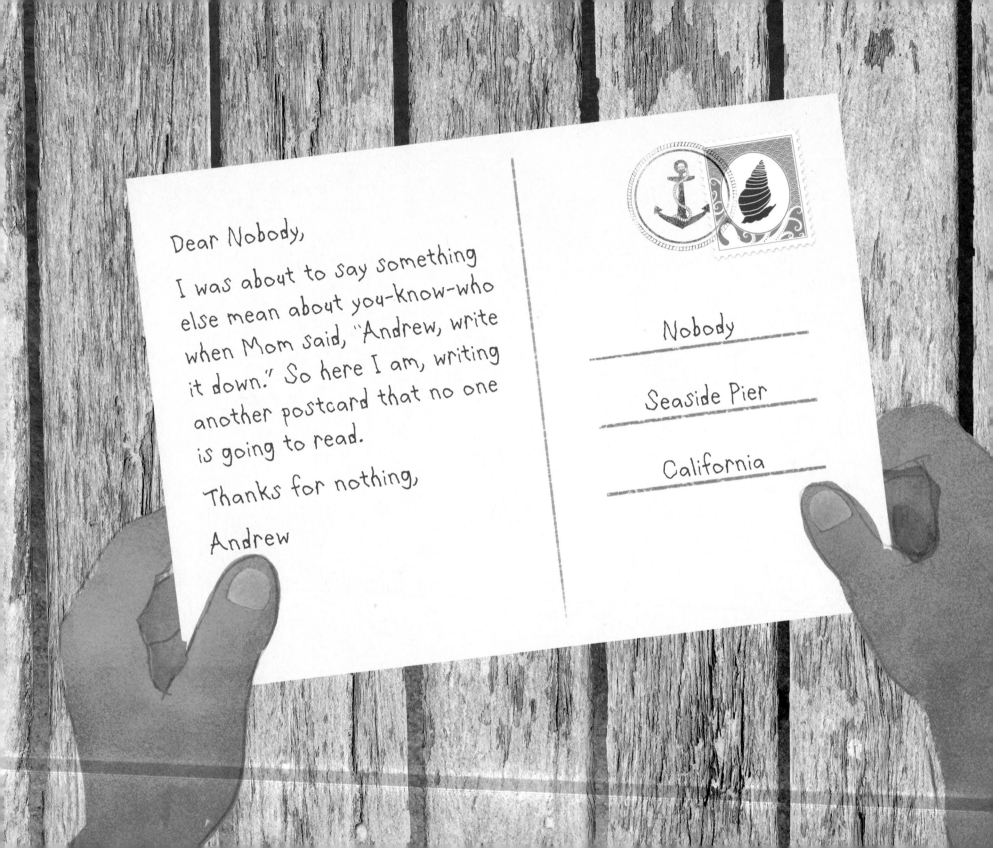

Dear Nobody,

I was about to say something else mean about you-know-who when Mom said, "Andrew, write it down." So here I am, writing another postcard that no one is going to read.

Thanks for nothing,

Andrew

Nobody

Seaside Pier

California

Agnes stroked her growing eggs. She
blew on them ever so gently. Her skin
turned from bumpy orange to creamy pink
as she wrote her reply.

Dear Andrew,

My name is AGNES. I may not be the smartest octopus in the sea, but I have read both your postcards. Have you ever tried swimming? You can't be mad or sad when you're swimming. Try it.

Sincerely,

Happy Agnes

Andrew

Above the Waves

California

Agnes sucker-kissed the eggs. She wiped away algae. They wouldn't be eggs much longer. It was time to send them a message.

Dear Eggs,

I can't believe how fast you're growing! You are my beautiful, breathing treasure. I wish we could stay like this forever.

Love,

Agnes

My Eggs

Old Rock Pile

Beneath the Pier

And then one day . . . they hatched!

Agnes waved as the babies floated away—forever.
Quickly, she scribbled them one last postcard.

Dear Beautiful Babies,

Watch out for crabs! And other octopuses. (Some of them think they are SO SMART.) If you find the perfect home, make sure it's empty before you move in. And then? Hunt. Sleep. Swim! Remember: You are the reason for everything.

Love,

Agnes

My Beautiful Babies

Pacific Ocean

California

Now Agnes's job was done. Like a ghost, she faded to white. But not before another postcard drifted her way.

Dear Agnes,

That first note in the bottle? It wasn't meant for you. (Shh. It was for my brother, Jack Henry.) You're not a monster at all—you're a hunter, a magician, a transformer! And guess what? I looked it up— you have THREE hearts! Thank you for writing to me.

Your friend,

Andrew

P.S. Swimming lessons start next week. Jack Henry isn't so bad in the pool.

Agnes

Pacific Ocean

California

Agnes swelled.
She swayed. She
knew exactly what
she wanted to say.

Dear World,

What a life, what a place! I have friends above the waves! And now I must say goodbye . . . GOODBYE! Don't worry, the end is not at all like I thought it would be. (You'll see.)

Gratefully,

Agnes Octopus

P.S. Hey, Andrew, give Jack Henry an octopus-sized hug—from ME.

The Whole World

More about Octopuses

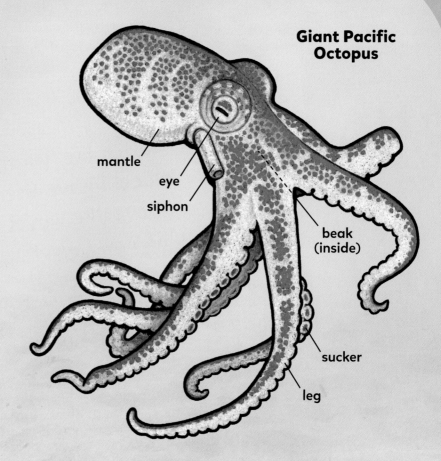

Giant Pacific Octopus

mantle

eye

siphon

beak (inside)

sucker

leg

Octopuses Are Complex, Fascinating Creatures

The octopus in this story is a giant Pacific octopus, which is the largest of about three hundred octopus species and lives in the cold waters of the Pacific Ocean. Its scientific name is *Enteroctopus dofleini*.

While Agnes lives just beneath a northwestern American coastal pier, other octopuses of this species can live in depths of up to 5,000 feet (1,500 m).

Just like Agnes, all giant Pacific octopuses live alone and hunt in darkness. They like to move around and seldom stay in one home for more than a couple of weeks (except when they are nesting).

You can often recognize an octopus den by the crab shells scattered near the entrance.

There's More to an Octopus Than Arms

These animals are amazingly fast growing: they hatch from eggs the size of a grain of rice, and during its three- to four-year life span, an octopus can grow to weigh as much as an adult human. An octopus's arms, when stretched tip to tip, can span the width of a car.

Scientists call octopuses cephalopods because of the way their feet (arms) are attached to their heads. Cephalopods are members of the mollusk family, which includes animals like squid, snails, and cuttlefish.

Octopuses have three hearts—two to pump blood through each of the two gills and a third to circulate blood throughout the body.

Their blood is blue. That's because in octopus bodies, copper carries the oxygen, not iron.

Their skin, which feels like a rubber glove, is constantly changing color and texture. It ranges from bumpy red when an octopus is excited to ghostly white when it is relaxed.

When an octopus gets old, its skin fades to shades of gray and white, and it no longer attacks prey.

Octopus bodies are 90 percent muscle and have no bones.

Each of its eight arms has two rows of suckers, and one sucker on an adult octopus can lift as much as 30 pounds (14 kg). And each sucker has about ten thousand neurons, making these arms extremely sensitive. Octopuses can even *taste* with their suckers!

An octopus has a beak, much like a parrot's.

They use their beaks to drill into their prey and deposit venom. This helps to stun the prey, making it easier for an octopus to catch and eat its meal.

They sometimes "ink," or squirt fluid to create cloudy water, to confuse predators and allow for fast escapes.

Reproduction Is Serious Business for an Octopus

Male octopuses live only about two months after mating. Meanwhile, the female searches for a place to lay her eggs. This is the female octopus's last most important job. Since females can lay up to one hundred thousand eggs, it is a huge undertaking!

The eggs take about six months to grow and develop before they hatch. Some mothers are so diligent that they don't leave the nest at all during this time, not even to eat. By the time the eggs hatch, the mother is too weak to defend herself or to hunt. One cell at a time, her body begins to dwindle and die.

When they hatch, baby octopuses are fully formed and instinctively know how to feed themselves. As they float off on the current, the biggest danger is the possibility of getting eaten by fish, crabs, or other marine life. Survivors grow and mate, and the cycle repeats itself again and again.

An Octopus Is Smarter Than It Looks

Octopuses are known to be highly intelligent, with brains that are huge compared to other cephalopods— an adult octopus's brain is about the size of a walnut.

They are notorious escape artists and can ooze through openings no bigger than a quarter.

They love hiding in bottles, cans, or other safe places.

In his book *The Toilers of the Sea*, Victor Hugo famously described an octopus as a monster "supple as leather, tough as steel, and cold as night." However, octopuses are not a threat to humans.

Octopuses have personalities—some are friendly, some are shy. Nearly all are incredibly curious—just like humans.

If You Want to Talk about More Than One Octopus

Agnes would like you to know that although *octopi* is widely used as the plural form of octopus, scientists use the word *octopuses*.

Further Reading

Books

Jay, Alison. *Out of the Blue*. Cambridge, MA: Barefoot Books, 2014.
When a giant octopus washes ashore during a big storm, a boy and girl, with the assistance of other marine animals, must find a way to return him to the sea.

Mather, Jennifer A., Roland C. Anderson, and James B. Wood. *Octopus: The Ocean's Intelligent Invertebrate*. Portland, OR: Timber, 2010.
Three leading marine biologists offer a wealth of information about octopuses, accompanied by color photographs.

Pringle, Laurence. *Octopuses! Strange and Wonderful*. Honesdale, PA: Boyds Mills, 2015.
Did you know that octopuses can change color to camouflage themselves? What about the fact that they can detach one of their arms to escape from predators? This book explores the oddities that make the octopus a unique and fascinating creature.

Riggs, Kate. *Octopuses*. Mankato, MN: Creative Education/Creative Paperbacks, 2016.
This photo-filled book covers a wide variety of topics, including the physical characteristics, habitat, behavior, and life cycle of the octopus.

Schuh, Mari. *The Supersmart Octopus*. Minneapolis: Lerner Publications, 2019.
This book looks at how octopuses use their smarts to hunt, avoid predators, navigate mazes, unlock jars, and more.

Websites

Octopus
https://kids.nationalgeographic.com/animals/octopus/#octopus
Learn more about how octopuses move, what they eat, and where they live, and check out links to additional photos and videos.

Octopus Fact Sheet
https://www.seattleaquarium.org/octopus
This site provides interesting facts about giant Pacific octopuses as well as a video of a diver releasing an octopus into Puget Sound in Seattle, Washington.

Why We're Suckers for the Giant Pacific Octopus
https://www.youtube.com/watch?v=CYK2i2tR7gU
In this video, an aquarium biologist at the Monterey Bay Aquarium in California shares his experiences working with a giant Pacific octopus.